Song Bird

by TOLOLWA M. MOLLEL

Illustrated by ROSANNE LITZINGER

CLARION BOOKS/New York

Clarion Books
a Houghton Mifflin Company imprint
215 Park Avenue South
New York, NY 10003
Text copyright © 1999 by Tololwa M. Mollel
Illustrations copyright © 1999 by Rosanne Litzinger

The illustrations for this book were executed in
fine watercolors and colored pencil.
The text is set in 16/22-point Mendoza.

Printed in Singapore.

Library of Congress Cataloging-in-Publication Data

Mollel, Tololwa M. (Tololwa Marti)
Song bird / by Tololwa M. Mollel ; illustrated by Rosanne Litzinger.
p.   cm.
Summary: An adaptation of a folktale from southern Africa, in which a
magical bird helps a kind young girl get back her people's stolen cattle from
Makucha the monster.
ISBN 0-395-82908-9
[1. Folklore—Tanzania.] I. Litzinger, Rosanne, ill. II. Title.
PZ8.1.M73So   1999
398.2'.09678'04528—dc21   98-22690
CIP
AC

TWP 10 9 8 7 6 5 4 3 2 1

To my wife, Obianuju, for her infectious love of song and dance.
—*T.M.M.*

And many thanks to Dinah Stevenson of Clarion Books
for her sensitive and brilliant use of her pencil on my stories over the years.

To Presley,
neighbor and friend.
—*R.L.*

There once was a land with so many cattle it was called Kung'ombe—land of countless cattle. But one night they all disappeared.

Without their cattle, life became hard for the people of Kung'ombe, including Mariamu and her parents.

"Now that we have no milk to sell at the market, we'll have to grow more food," Mariamu's father said.

Early one morning, Mariamu and her parents
went to clear a wild, overgrown field. They felled
trees, burned bushes, dug up weeds, and hoed the
earth soft for sowing. They worked and worked.

At dusk, while her parents headed home, Mariamu
stayed back to pick wild berries. Suddenly, a little
bird landed nearby on the cleared field and began
to sing:

> *Kwa dem di mola kwa dem di mola*
> *Nyasi rejeeni kwa dem di mola*
> *Vichaka rudini kwa dem di mola*
> *Miti inukeni kwa dem di mola*
> *Haya haya haya kwa dem di mola.*

Mariamu watched in astonishment as all the dug-up weeds, the burned bushes, and the felled trees returned to the cleared field. "What have you done!" Mariamu exclaimed.

"This is my field, home to my eggs," replied the bird. "I know why you cleared it. Look, if you promise never to clear it again, I'll give you all the milk you want."

"Milk!" cried Mariamu. "I haven't had a drop of it since the night all our cattle vanished. I promise we'll leave your field alone if you'll give us milk."

Mariamu took the bird home and told her parents all that had happened.

Then the bird sang:

Kwa dem di mola kwa dem di mola
Maziwa maziwa kwa dem di mola
Churu-churuzika kwa dem di mola
Tiri-tiririka kwa dem di mola
Haya haya haya kwa dem di mola.

At once, all their gourds filled with milk. Mariamu's parents could hardly believe it.

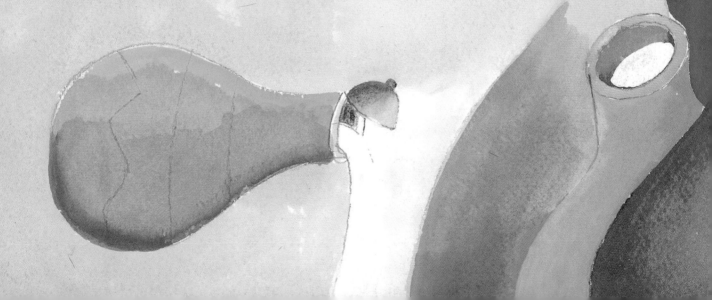

The next morning Mariamu woke up to find the bird in a cage. "You can't cage the bird," she protested. "She has been so kind to us."

Mariamu's parents had other ideas.

"Think of all the milk she'll give us if we keep her," said her mother.

"We'd be fools to let her go!" said her father.

Excited, they loaded their donkeys with gourds of milk, and the three of them set out for market. They hadn't gone far when Mariamu announced she had to go back and change her headdress.

At home Mariamu quickly freed the bird, who thanked her and said, "For your kindness I would like to reward you." And the bird broke into song. Instantly, to her great surprise, Mariamu shrank to the size of a worm. Then the bird told her, "Fasten yourself to my leg with your headdress and hold on tight. We're going on a journey."

"Where?" Mariamu asked eagerly.

"To a place you have never been," the bird answered, and flew out.

They flew over empty corrals and pastures, over cropland, and over plains stretching as far as the eye could see.

By and by they came to a strange land where everything was dozens of times bigger than normal. Instead of the sun, a huge moon shone down brightly. Mariamu gasped. "It's night!" she said in wonder.

"It's always night in Makucha's land," said the bird.

"Makucha? Who is Makucha?"

"A monster," replied the bird. "He's the one who made your cattle vanish. He brought them here."

Soon the bird and Mariamu came to a forest of giant trees. At the edge of the forest, they perched on the top branch of a fig tree tall as a mountain. Mariamu looked down across the plains. She saw a dusty endless sea of trotting cattle, herded along by jackals. Pointing at the lumbering figure behind the approaching cattle, Mariamu exclaimed, "Look, Makucha the monster!"

The bird nodded. "Taking the cattle home from pasture. We'll follow him to his compound and get the cattle back."

"How?"

Before the bird could answer, the ground shook.

Araka raka
Toto ko Makucha
Toto ko Makucha!

19

As the jackals came racing toward them, the bird and Mariamu flew to a bush. There the bird taunted Makucha, who lunged at them and missed. The bird perched on another bush. Makucha followed, chanting:

Araka raka
Dege ko Makucha
Dege ko Makucha!

The night resounded with the baying of jackals, the bird's taunting squawks, Mariamu's terrified shrieks, and Makucha's furious pursuit of the bird from bush to bush.

Finally the bird flew to the forest and perched out of reach on the top branch of the mountain-tall fig tree. The next moment the tree began to shake, *tim tim tim*, and Mariamu cried out, "He's cutting down the tree!"

Far below, wood chips sprayed from the trunk as Makucha chopped wildly through the tree with his sword-nails. But the bird only laughed, and when the tree began to fall, she sang:

> *Kwa dem di mola kwa dem di mola*
> *Vipisi rudini kwa dem di mola*
> *Rejea mkongani kwa dem di mola*
> *Imarisha mti kwa dem di mola*
> *Haya haya haya kwa dem di mola.*

All the wood chips flew back into the trunk. The tree stopped falling and stood stronger and straighter than ever. Time and again Makucha chopped through the tree. Time and again, with Mariamu singing along merrily, the bird sang the tree strong and straight.

One by one, Makucha's sword-nails were worn down by the trunk of the fig tree. With every nail he lost, the monster grew weaker and weaker. Finally, Makucha's hands dropped to his sides, and he toppled over with a ground-shaking thud. The jackals milled around his sprawled figure, howling helplessly.

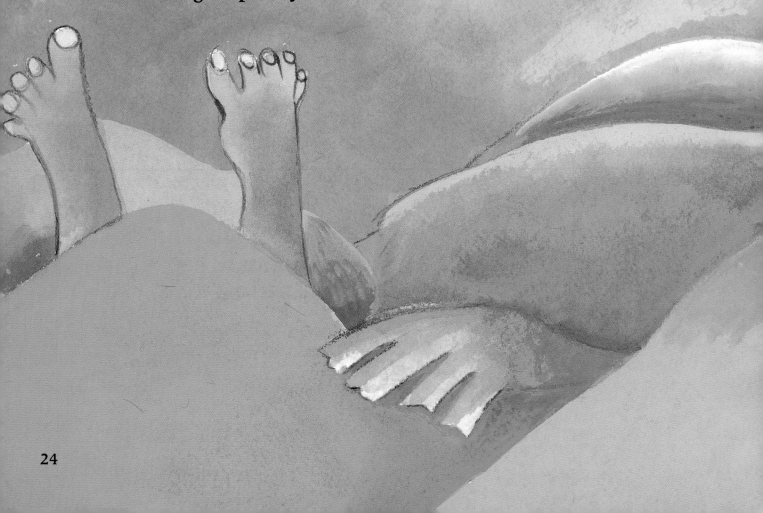

"It will be a long time before Makucha's nails grow and he gets his power back," the bird said to Mariamu. "Let's go and fetch the cattle."

At Makucha's compound, the bird sang Mariamu back to her normal size. Quickly, the girl let the cattle out of the corral.

"I'll sing all of us back home," the bird said.

The return of Mariamu and the missing cattle brought joy to everyone in Kung'ombe. None was happier, or more relieved, than Mariamu's parents. They were amazed to hear their daughter's breathless account of her journey. At a big homecoming ceremony, they thanked the bird and promised never again to clear that one field.

After the ceremony, the bird bid everyone good-bye. "I have other fields with eggs to protect," she told Mariamu.

No one ever saw the little bird again. But Mariamu and her parents kept their promise and never again cleared the field, which they named Field of the Song Bird.

From wherever she was, the Song Bird rewarded them for a promise honored. The next rainy season was the best Mariamu could remember. The earth glistened with the wildest bloom of fresh grass. The cattle calved as never before. Field of the Song Bird abounded with the liveliest and most colorful birds ever seen in Kung'ombe.

And as she did the milking, Mariamu sang:

Kwa dem di mola kwa dem di mola
Maziwa maziwa kwa dem di mola
Churu-churuzika kwa dem di mola
Tiri-tiririka kwa dem di mola
Haya haya haya kwa dem di mola.

Author's Note

Song Bird is my adaptation of a traditional story about a magical bird and a monster. The story is found in different versions among the Zulu and Xhosa and other ethnic groups in southern Africa, including southern Tanzania. In my adaptation, I have amplified some of the story's traditional themes and added a few of my own, modifying the role and character of the bird and the monster. Setting the story in Tanzania, I made up a Swahili song for the bird and borrowed a traditional Tanzanian tune and refrain. Makucha's chant is in bad Swahili, as befits his monster image. I have also made up some words for sounds: *birim* (bee REAM), the sound of empty gourds rolling; *gulum* (goo LOOM), swallowing; *kiram* (key RUM), Makucha's footsteps shaking the earth; *ngurum* (ng goo ROOM), the rolling of gourds full of milk; and *tim* (TEE mm), tree shaking from Makucha's sword-nail strokes.

Transcribed by Paul Alan Levi

araka raka (ah RAH kah RAH kah): quick, quick (monster's bad Swahili) • *chafyaaa* (CHA fyaaah): a sneeze; sound of an explosive sneeze • *churu-churuzika* (choo roo choo roo zee KAH): dri-drip out • *dege ko Makucha* (DEH geh koh Makucha): bring birdie to Makucha (bad Swahili) • *haya haya haya* (ha YAH ha YAH ha YAH): hurry hurry hurry • *imarisha mti* (EE ma ree shah mm TEE): make the tree strong • **Kung'ombe** (KOONG ohm beh): land of countless cattle • *kwa dem di mola* (qua DEHM dee moh la): something like "tra la la . . ." • **Makucha** (Ma KOO chah): Mr. Long Nails • **Mariamu** (Ma ree ah MOO): a Tanzanian girl's name • *masiwa* (ma SEE wah) *ko Makucha* : bring milk to Makucha (bad Swahili) • *maziwa maziwa* (ma ZEE wah ma ZEE wah): milk milk • *miti inukeni* (me tee EE noo keh nee): trees get up, arise • *nyasi rejeeni* (nyah SI reh jeh EH nee): weeds come back • *rejea mkongani* (reh jeh AH mm KOHN gah nee): go back into the trunk • *tiri-tiririka* (tee ree tee ree ree KAH): flo-flow out • *toto* (TOH toh) *ko Makucha* : bring the little one to Makucha (bad Swahili) • *vichaka rudini* (vee CHAH kah roo DEE nee): bushes come back • *vipisi rudini* (vee PEA see roo DEE nee): wood chips come back